Scrum!

by

Tom Palmer

Illustrated by Dylan Gibson

To my Aunty Margaret, who lives in one of the great rugby towns, Warrington.

Thanks to David Luxton and Rebecca Palmer for helping with the book.

First published in 2011 in Great Britain by
Barrington Stoke Ltd
18 Walker St, Edinburgh, EH3 7LP

www.barringtonstoke.co.uk

ISBN: 978-1-84299-944-8

Printed in China by Leo

Contents

Foreword

This story is about a boy who struggles with hard choices. He feels he has to choose between two dads, two homes and two rugby codes. Tom Palmer has worked hard to make sure the book is easy to read, because some people struggle with reading.

I struggled with reading when I was young and even when I got a bit older, because I'm dyslexic. I was a bit like Steven in the book – I tried to cope on my own. Also like Steven, I found out that it always helps to speak to someone when you've got a problem. Now I work with a charity called Dyslexia Action. They help kids and adults get to grips with reading, so if you know anyone who finds it hard, spread the word. Then they can read great books about rugby too – and other things they like.

Keep reading and keep playing!

Kenny Logan

Kenny Logan is a Rugby Union legend who won over 70 caps in his career. He is the patron of Dyslexia Action.

This book is about two types of rugby – Rugby League and Rugby Union. To find out more about them, turn to page 72!

Chapter 1
BMW

Steven Webb timed his run just right.

Half the players were in a scrum round the ball. They threw it out and his mate Nash got hold of it. Nash threw it to Steven just as Steven got to the perfect speed to catch it.

Now he had to get past three tackles.

The first tackle was easy. Steven slowed his pace right down, then jumped over the arms of the prop who was there to stop him.

In the second tackle the other player got hold of Steven's legs but Steven was stronger. He carried on running and the other player slipped down his legs and let go.

One more tackle to face and Steven would score the try that would win the game.

Steven saw the other player come from the left. He stepped up his pace until he was running fast. Very fast.

That was all it took. Pace.

The other player, a winger, was left behind. He was so far behind that Steven could run back to the middle and dive over the goal line between the posts.

They won the game.

“That was fantastic, son,” said Steven’s dad in the car on the way back to Leeds after the game. He was on a high.

“You were the best player on that pitch by a mile,” his dad went on. “It’s only a matter of time before some club comes and snaps you up. Some Super League club.”

Steven smiled and looked at his dad. He loved this. His dad was so sure that one day Steven would be a famous Rugby League player.

They were on the way to Steven’s mum’s house. It was what they did every Saturday. His dad would collect him, take him to the game, then leave him at his mum’s afterwards.

His mum and dad had split up when Steven was four. He was 14 now, but he saw them both almost every day. Even though they lived apart, they were still friends.

In fact Steven still hoped they'd get back together one day, even though he would never say. He was sure his dad wanted that.

"Will you come in and tell Mum about the game?" Steven asked.

"Sure," Dad said, with a grin.

But when the car turned off the main road, Steven felt it stop with a jolt as his dad hit the brake.

"What's up?" Steven asked.

He saw his dad look at the parking space in front of the house.

There was another car there. A BMW.

"Is that *his* car?" Dad asked in a low voice.

Steven nodded.

“Then I’m not coming in.”

Chapter 2
Big News

"Alright, love," Mum said. She was at the door the moment Steven opened it.

Steven knew why she had come to the door: she wanted to stop his dad before he saw her boyfriend. Her BMW-driving boyfriend Martin.

"Isn't your dad coming in?" she asked.

"No," Steven said, with a look back through the door. "He saw Martin's car in the drive."

Mum looked angry for a second but then she smiled.

"Come in," she said in a loud voice so Steven's dad could hear. "Martin's inside."

Steven followed her into the front room.

"Hello, Steve," Martin said. He stood up and came to shake Steven's hand. "How was the game tonight? Did you win?"

Steven could have smiled but he didn't.

He hated the way Martin called him Steve and the funny way he shook his hand. But he *liked* the way Martin always asked about his rugby. Mum's last boyfriend couldn't have cared less about it. At least Martin looked like he wanted to know.

"Yes, thanks," Steven answered. He hadn't sat down yet.

"Did you score?"

"Two tries."

"Well done, Steve. I'll have to come and see you play some day."

As they spoke, Steven saw his mum close the front room door. Steven knew his mum. If she wanted the door closed it meant they were going to have a talk. A big talk.

"Sit down, Steven," Mum said.

Steven sat. He had a good idea what this was about.

"Me and Martin have something to tell you," Mum said. Her voice was funny. Nervous.

"Yeah?" Steven said.

"It's not easy to say," said Mum, "but ..." She stopped.

Steven cut in. "You're getting married."

Mum looked shocked. "How did you know?"

Steven shrugged.

"Your son's not stupid," Martin said to Steven's mum.

Steven didn't want to smile but he was a bit pleased that Martin thought he was smart.

"I'm pleased for you," Steven said, after a second. "I hope you'll both be happy."

"Thank you," Mum and Martin said together.

But Mum didn't look happy.

Steven stood up. "I need a bath," he said. To tell the truth, he needed time to think.

"Wait," Mum said. "There's more to tell you."

"What?" Steven asked.

"You'd better sit down," Mum said.

This time, Steven had no idea what they had to tell him. He looked at their faces. They looked even more nervous.

Steven tried to think of something funny to say. "You don't want me to be a bridesmaid, do you?"

Steven's mum laughed. She laughed a little bit too much.

Then she spoke.

"We have to move," she said. "You and me, with Martin. Down south."

Chapter 3
Kicking Off

Steven slipped out of the back door and closed it without a sound. He didn't want to have to say he was going out, or to face his mum's worries. He just needed to clear his head. To think.

He picked up his rugby ball on the way out. The one his dad had bought him at the Leeds club shop.

A good kick-about. That was what would help him wind down.

Steven walked out of his street, across the main road, onto the sports field and over to the rugby posts. He could kick some goals. No one would be there – it was almost dark now.

Thirty yards out he made a hole in the grass with the heel of his boot. Then he stood the ball in it.

He stepped back one, two, three long steps. The stretch in the back of his legs felt good.

Two steps to the side. Just like he'd seen Jonny Wilkinson do.

Then he looked at the posts, taking in the view. There were two white posts and a row of trees, dark against the dying light in the sky.

As he got ready to kick the ball, he saw two people walk towards him. But it didn't distract him.

One, two, three, he hit the ball. It looped the 30 yards, hit the left post and bounced in. Perfect.

He stood still as he saw one of the people bend down to pick up the ball and drop kick it back to him.

It was Craig and Sam. Two mates from school.

"You're out late," Sam said.

"So are you," Steven said.

Steven saw Sam smile. They were good mates. He felt a deep need to tell them about the move.

Once he had said it, Steven watched to see what they would do.

Craig spoke first. "They're all soft down south."

"Yeah," said Steven. "That's what I heard."

"They speak like this," Craig said, trying to sound like he was in *EastEnders*.

Steven watched Sam laugh. Then Sam's face changed to shock as he took it in. "What about the rugby?" Sam asked.

Steven looked at him. "What about it?"

Sam stared at him. "They play Union."

Steven nodded. "I heard that too. But they're letting me keep on playing up here. On Saturdays."

"They're stuck up, too," Craig said. "They think they're better than us."

"That'll never work," Sam said, at the same time. "How will you train?"

Steven said nothing. All the thoughts that had been racing around in his head for the last half hour had now been put into words by his mates.

His life was a disaster. He'd never felt so low.

Chapter 4
Home and Away

"This is your room, Steve."

Steven looked past Martin and into the room. It was big. Very big. This was a very posh house.

And Martin was doing everything he could to make Steven feel at home.

Since they had left home Martin had not stopped making promises. The main one was that Steven would not have to miss any training or games back in Leeds.

"I've worked it out," Martin said. "If you get the 7 o'clock train from Grantham, you can be in Leeds for 8.30. I'll drive you to Grantham."

Steven knew that that meant Martin would have to get up at 5 am every Saturday and drive for two hours. And he would have to pay for the train tickets. They were big promises.

"Thanks," he said. But that was all he could say.

Martin showed Steven round his new bedroom. A 32-inch TV screen sat in pride of place in the corner.

"It's got all the Sky Sports channels," Martin said. "And movies."

There was also a PS3 and an X-Box 360.

"Thanks," Steven said again. He wanted to sound happy but he couldn't. He was miserable.

He felt as if his guts had been ripped out. He was nearly 200 miles from home. Everyone spoke different, looked different, lived in different houses and even played different rugby. He was away from his mates, his rugby team and – worst of all – his dad.

And he knew that his dad would be feeling bad about it too. Very bad. Bad that Steven wasn't near him. Bad that Steven was away from Rugby League in the north, in the land of Rugby Union in the south.

So, however many promises Martin made, however many things he bought, Steven wouldn't be happy.

There was really nothing Martin could do. Steven almost felt sorry for him.

Just then Martin cut into Steven's thoughts. "So, how about we go and watch a match tomorrow night?" he said.

"That's a great idea," Mum said.

Steven wasn't sure. Maybe Martin meant a football match.

"Saints are playing," Martin went on.

Steven thought for a second. "But that's Rugby Union," he said. "I can't go to that."

"Why not?" Mum said. She sounded cross with Steven for the first time since they'd left Yorkshire.

Steven didn't want to go because he knew how his dad would feel about it. But there was no way Steven could tell Mum and Martin that.

"I just can't," he said again.

Chapter 5
Day One, New School

Steven's new school looked more like a palace. There were towers and turrets glowing in the morning sun.

"It's a very old school," Mum said.

"Yeah?" Steven said. He was too nervous to chat.

"Are you sure you don't want me to come in with you?" asked his mum.

"I'm sure."

Steven knew he'd snapped. But his mum smiled as he climbed out of the car and joined the lines of pupils walking towards the school.

A boy came over to Steven. "You must be Steve," he said with a smile. He was tall and thin, but strong-looking.

He'd be a good winger, Steven thought before he could stop himself.

"It's Steven," Steven said, "not Steve."

"Sorry," the boy said. "Steven. I'm Josh. And this is James."

Another boy stood at Josh's side. He was short and dark haired. Stocky.

He'd be a prop, Steven thought.

“We just wanted to say that if you need help to settle in, you can ask us,” said Josh.

Steven saw James nod.

“A new school and all that,” Josh went on, “it must be pretty hard.”

“Yes,” Steven said. “And thanks. I’ve got to go to register at somewhere called the Court. Do you know where it is?”

“I’ll take you,” James said. “It’s not far.”

They walked along a wide hall with wood panels on the walls. Steven couldn’t believe that this was a normal school. It was dead posh.

“So you’re from Leeds?” James asked. “Do you support Leeds United?”

“Sort of,” Steven said, “but I’m more into rugby.”

"Great," James said. "Me too."

As they talked, Steven heard heavy footsteps behind him. He looked round and saw a large man.

"You OK, James?" the man said.

Steven thought he'd seen the man somewhere before, but he couldn't work out where.

"Yes, Mr Evans," said Josh. "This is Steven Webb. He's new today."

"Ah, yes," Mr Evans said. "Martin's lad?"

Steven didn't hear what the teacher said because he had just remembered where he had seen him before. It was Barry Evans, the former Welsh rugby star.

"Sorry?" said Steven.

"Are you Martin Taylor's lad?"

"Er, yeah," Steven said, even though he felt funny about being called that.

"Martin tells me you're a very good player. We'd love it if you would like to try out for the school team. What do you think?"

Steven felt like he was about to snap. There were too many things going on in his head all at once. But he knew he had to be careful what he said. This was a teacher, after all.

"I still play for a Rugby League team in Leeds," he said, thinking of his dad and how he would feel if Steven started to play for a Rugby Union team.

"Oh, well," said Mr Evans with a smile, "if you change your mind ..."

Chapter 6
Sixth Tackle

Steven had felt very odd during his first morning at the new school. The place was different. The voices were different. And it seemed that they learned different things, even though the lessons were meant to be the same.

By the afternoon, things had started to look up.

That was because the afternoon meant Games. Or sport, as they called it in Steven's old school.

But it didn't matter what it was called. It meant rugby.

Steven knew that playing Rugby Union would be odd. But he'd seen enough Six Nations' Rugby to know what to do. And this wasn't like playing in a real match: it was just a Games lesson.

He noticed that Mr Evans had put Josh and James on his team, so he knew he was with mates.

And it did go well. He kept out of the rucks, when lots of players from each team would fight over the ball on the ground after it had been got out of a tackle. He didn't get into the mauls, when they would push a player from all sides to try and get the ball. Instead he watched and waited for a pass and tried to understand the rules. Any time he got the ball he made good use of it. He was so fast no one could tackle him and he got the ball much nearer the other team's goal.

It was going well.

Half way through the lesson he got the ball and wanted to make something happen. A pass had come to him six yards from the line and after the fifth tackle. That meant he had to kick, pass or get the ball over the line. He couldn't afford for any player to get him down on the ground.

But there was no time, no space. And he was tackled.

He let go of the ball, angry with himself.

"What are you doing?" James shouted.

"What?" Steven said.

"Why did you release the ball?"

"Sixth tackle," Steven said. As soon as he had said it he knew he had been a fool. There was no sixth tackle in Rugby Union. That was a Rugby *League* rule.

Steven wanted everyone to forget about his mistake so instead of playing safe, he decided to run with the ball and attack everything.

And it paid off.

He scored three tries. The third time was the last move of the game. Steven ran wider and wider, always changing speed so no one could tackle him.

When he planted the ball on the ground, he heard the whistle and saw Mr Evans, the rugby hero, jog over to him.

Mr Evans held out a hand to help Steven up. As he did, he spoke so only Steven could hear.

"You've got to change your mind, Steven," Mr Evans said, "even though you don't know Rubgy Union, you have the most talent in this school."

"When's the next game?" Steven asked. He was dead excited and pleased.

"Friday," Mr Evans said. "Friday night."

Chapter 7
Bitter-sweet

As the train raced north on Saturday morning Steven rubbed his sore legs. The game the night before had been hard. There were different things you had to do in Rugby Union. You had to push more. There was less time to stop and recover. He'd had to put a lot in.

But it had gone well. Very well. He'd scored 18 points in a 27-22 victory. His team mates and Mr Evans were all over him at the end.

But Steven felt it now.

Every time the train bumped his sore legs he felt like it was the pain of hurting his dad. The good memories of the night before were all bitter-sweet. How Josh and James had carried him off the pitch as a joke. How Mr Evans had praised him. How much fun it had been.

He felt even worse when he got to Leeds.

He wasn't even off the train when his dad lifted him up in a giant hug. This was the first time they'd seen each other since the move south. He knew his dad would have missed him.

"Great to see you, Steven," Dad said.

"Hello, Dad."

It was good to see his mates again too. Even if they made fun of him at first, saying he didn't sound like he was from the north and he was now posh.

But the game wasn't good. Before they were half way through the first half Steven was shattered. The night before had caught up with him.

Why had he thought he could play two games in 24 hours?

He did his best to play on but it was useless. His dad spotted it straight away. He said so after the game.

"What's up?"

"Nothing," Steven said.

"Have you not trained this week?"

"Didn't get a chance," Steven said. It wasn't a total lie. He'd not had the chance to train for Rugby *League*.

"Are you ill?" asked his dad.

"I'm not sure."

Steven was scared his dad would ask him straight. *Have you been playing Rugby Union?* Then he'd *have* to lie.

"It's the move, lad, I'm sorry," his dad said. He put his arm round Steven, who was pleased he didn't have to talk any more. "You've had a right week of it," his dad went on. "You'll get it back, don't worry."

"Yeah," Steven agreed.

"You'd better, anyway," Dad went on, "it's the final next week. There'll be Super League scouts there."

Chapter 8
County Call Up

Back in the south Steven spent a week settling into life in his new school. He went out to see a film with Josh and James. He started to put his hand up in class. He even watched a Rugby Union game on TV with Martin. It was OK.

But everything became much *more* OK after another game for the school.

Mr Evans waved to Steven to join him as Steven walked off the pitch. Mr Evans was with another man.

"Steven," Mr Evans said. "Great game. Well done."

"Thanks, Mr Evans."

The other man put his hand out to Steven. Steven shook it.

"This is David Lane," said Mr Evans. "He's the coach for the county team. I asked him to come and have a look at you."

"Me?" said Steven.

"Yes," said Mr Evans. "You."

"But I've only just begun."

"That's right," David Lane said with a nod. "You are only going to get better. A lot better. It's too early in your Rugby Union career to invite you to play any games yet at county level, but we would love it if you would come and train with us."

Steven frowned. "What does *county level* mean?"

"It means you would play for Northamptonshire, son," David Lane said. "The next step after that is to play for England."

Chapter 9
The George Hotel

Steven travelled up the night before the final in the north because his dad said he had sorted somewhere special in Huddersfield for them to stay.

All the way he tried to make up his mind if he should tell his dad about his chance to train with the county Rugby Union team.

On the one hand, he thought his dad would be proud of his son playing at such a high level.

On the other hand, he thought his dad would be angry at his son playing Rugby Union.

He met his dad in Leeds and they got the train to Huddersfield.

"So where are we staying?" Steven asked.

"It's a surprise."

Steven was getting nervous about the game. He wanted to make sure his body was right. "I want to get some rest before the game," he said. "A good night's sleep."

"You'll get the best night's sleep you've ever had," his dad said. "Trust me."

Steven didn't ask any more questions.

"There'll be Super League scouts at the final," Dad said as they passed through Dewsbury.

"Yeah, you told me before," Steven said. He was busy trying not to think about Rugby Union. At least not until after the game. That was his focus right now. The next game.

They got off the train at Huddersfield and walked out of the station into a square.

His dad stopped. "There you are," he said.

"What?" Steven asked. He put his bag down. His dad pointed across the square.

"The George Hotel," he said.

"What?"

"That's where we're staying," said his dad. "The George Hotel."

Steven had not stayed in a hotel since they went on holiday before his mum and dad split up. He smiled and picked up his bag. "Cheers, Dad," he said.

Then he felt his dad's hand on his shoulder. He knew to put the bag down again.

"This isn't any old hotel, Steven."

"No?"

"This is the George Hotel in Huddersfield," said his dad. "Where Rugby League started. In 1895."

Steven remembered now. Over 100 years ago a group of northern rugby club owners had met here. They had decided to break away from Rugby Union and play their own

GEORGE HOTEL

game with their own rules here in the north. His dad had brought him here before.

"I want us to stay here tonight because I think you're on the verge of something great," his dad said. "Those scouts are coming to look at *you*. From Leeds, St Helens and Warrington. I want you to understand the history of Rugby League. Because you are about to become part of that history."

Chapter 10
Final

Steven did not sleep well. He woke up at least one time every hour with his head full of confused thoughts. He was scared that he would do a Rugby Union move and blow the game. In front of his dad. And all his mates.

And because he had not slept he was worried he'd be too tired to put in the kind of game his dad would want from him.

But the game went well. Very well. Better for Steven than anyone else.

He felt like he had something extra to his game. Each time his team were on the first or second tackle, he would attack. He knew not to play safe and lose the ball when there were four or five tackles to go. And he attacked hard. No one was expecting it.

By half time Steven had scored three tries. One time he had run right up the pitch while all his team's families cheered.

By full time he'd scored seven. And had converted them all. It was his best game ever.

He was a better player than he had ever been before. And he knew why. He'd learnt new skills in Rugby Union.

After all the cheers were over, they lifted the cup, listened to the speeches and shook hands with all the scouts. Steven was happy. He'd never felt this good. He stood and looked out across the pitch, at the holy ground and the shadows of the posts, with his dad's arm around him.

"You made it today," Dad said. "Any one of those clubs will have you now. They've all asked for my phone number. I'm so proud of you. I've missed you since your mum moved you away, but now I feel like you're back."

Steven smiled. This was good. Very good. Maybe this was the right thing for him. Maybe he should go with this. With Rugby League. That was his game. And his dad was happy, so he was happy too.

Then his dad's voice changed. Only a little. But it was different.

“There was something different about your game today,” his dad said.

Steven said nothing. He wanted to avoid the subject of Rugby Union.

But he knew his dad was onto him.

“It made me think of Scott Quinnell. When he came from Union to League. Remember?”

Steven didn’t want to keep telling lies to his dad. He was happy now, and pretty sure that Rugby League was for him.

“I’ve been playing down there,” he said in a rush, wanting to get it all out. “For school. A scout came to watch me there too. He asked me to train with the county team, but I’ve decided ...”

His dad cut him off. “You what? You’ve sold out? I can’t believe this. After all the years I've put in for you, you want to turn your back on everything I care about!"

His dad turned and stormed away. Then he stopped and turned to Steven again.

"Go on, go off back to that Martin and his posh car and his stuck up game. That's fine. So long as you're happy."

Steven walked to the station to get the train home. He didn't want to think about his dad or Martin or the south or the north or Rugby League or Rugby Union. His head was too sore. He felt sick. And he was sure that he never wanted to play rugby again in his life.

Chapter 11
Home

The week after, Steven was still sure that he would never play rugby again.

He'd left the school team.

He had not listened to any of the messages his dad had left on his phone.

He'd even taken his rugby posters off the wall.

He could tell his mum was worried. She would stand and watch him while he did his homework or played on his PS3. Then she would sigh.

When Steven's mum sighed he knew she wanted to say something, but she didn't know how. It drove him nuts, so he would look at her to dare her to say it. And that meant he had given her what she wanted.

"Why don't you call your dad, Steven?" she said one day after tea. Martin was putting the dishes into the dish-washer. He had not said anything about Steven's dad – which Steven kind of liked him for. He'd said nothing to Steven about how he'd stopped rugby at school either.

"I'm still angry with Dad," Steven said. "I'm not ready to speak to him."

"Steven, he's going out of his mind," Mum said. "He loves you. Just call him."

"Not yet," Steven said.

Martin went out into the hall. Steven heard him get his coat and his car keys. He was going to the rugby. Saints versus Wasps. And Steven knew that Martin would ask him if he'd like to come too. He always did.

And Steven always said no. Every time.

Martin came into the room.

"Right. I'm off," he said. "Steven, would you like to come?"

What Steven did then shocked himself. Maybe he didn't want to be stuck with his mum all night while she nagged him. Maybe he missed rugby. He wasn't sure. But he stood up.

"Yeah," he said. "I'll come."

The drive back from the game was good. Steven had loved seeing Rugby Union live. It had been a total rush. The crowd had been buzzing.

"When are Saints playing at home again?" he asked.

"Ten days," Martin said, and pressed his foot down to move away from a set of traffic lights. "Did you like it?"

"I did."

Steven was pleased that Martin left it at that. There was no pressure. No questions. No advice. He was starting to like Martin, much to his surprise.

Steven sat back and smiled. Maybe things were going to be OK. Maybe he could play rugby again. But, before that could happen, he had to sort something. He had to call his dad.

Steven felt his mobile in his pocket. When he was alone in his room at home he'd call him.

As Martin turned into their street, Steven saw something that made his heart cramp.

A car in the drive.

A blue Nissan.

His dad's blue Nissan.

Chapter 12
Upside Down

Steven went in to the house first, pushing the front door open and walking into the living room. He nearly fell over a rugby ball that he had left behind the door.

He heard his dad before he saw him. There was a sound of sobs coming from the room.

Mum was next to dad on the sofa, with her arm round him.

When his dad looked at him, Steven wasn't sure what to do. He had never seen his dad cry before. It felt like the world had turned upside down. Nothing was the same.

"Hi, Dad," he said after a second.

Dad stared at him.

"Come and sit down, Steven," Mum said.

And then she left them.

The room was so quiet Steven could hear his own heart beat. He didn't have a clue what to say to his dad, who had still not said anything.

In the end Steven said, "Are you OK?"

"I've been better," Dad said, trying to smile.

Steven smiled too.

Then his dad cleared his throat. "I've got something I need to say to you, son."

Steven shut his eyes. He was sure his dad would be angry. "Yeah?" he said.

"I want to say ... I'm sorry."

Steven opened his eyes. Then his dad put his arms round him and he closed them again.

"I'm sorry too," Steven said. His voice was swallowed up by his dad's jumper.

His dad pulled himself away. "What did you say?"

"I said I'm sorry too."

An hour later, they'd talked and talked and Steven's dad had told him all the news from home. Then Steven took him into the kitchen. Mum and Martin were sitting drinking cups of tea.

"Alright, Martin," Dad said.

Martin nodded. "Great, thanks. It's good to see you."

"You too," Dad said.

Steven went over to the kettle. "Cup of tea, Dad?"

"In a minute, maybe," Dad said. "I think I'd like a bit of fresh air." He stopped. "How about you, Martin?"

Steven stared at them. What was this all about?

Martin stood up. "Sure. I'll get my coat."

As the two men headed for the door, Steven moved to watch them. He saw Martin step over the ball that was still in the middle of the hall.

Then he saw his dad bend down, pick it up and tuck it under his arm.

The door closed behind them.

Chapter 13
Kicking

Steven wasn't sure what to do next.

He looked at his mum.

"Do you want to talk?" she asked.

Steven shook his head. "Not really. I think I'll go up to my room for a while."

"OK," Mum said.

In his room, Steven sat on the bed and stared at the bare walls where the posters used to be. The blinds were shut.

Now what?

He'd had a good talk with his dad. His dad had told him that he had had calls from Wigan, St Helens and Leeds Rhinos. All of them wanted to offer Steven a trial.

But he'd loved the Rugby Union game last night. And Martin was – and had always been – nice to him. And he had the chance of playing with the county Rugby Union team.

What should he do?

The one thing he did know was that he did want to play rugby.

But which code? League or Union?

As he thought about it, Steven heard a thump as someone kicked a rugby ball. *Some kids on the fields*, he thought.

He opened the blinds.

There were two guys kicking a rugby ball to each other on the fields. At first Steven didn't know who they were. They didn't look like any of the lads he knew here.

Then he looked again.

And he knew them.

The two men were standing 100 metres apart, kicking the ball to each other.

Steven watched as one of them drop kicked the ball high. It spun as it came down.

He saw the other man step to the side, move his feet, then catch the ball in his arms.

The first man was his dad.

The other one was Martin.

Steven smiled.

Two Codes, One Game

Rugby League and Rugby Union are both popular sports in the UK and many other countries. Rugby Union has been played for 200 years and Rugby League for over 100 years. The two sports split at a famous meeting in the George Hotel in Huddersfield, which is in the story.

In the UK, people play Rugby League mostly in the north of England, and they play Rugby Union mostly in the midlands and the south of England and in Wales and Scotland.

Rugby League has 13 players in each team and Rugby Union 15 players. They play with the same oval ball and with the same 'H' shaped goals at each end. They score points by scoring tries, where the ball is touched down over the try line, or kicking the ball between the posts.

Rugby Union and Rugby League both have scrums. This is where players from both sides push against each other to win the ball. They both also have tackles, where a player has to let go of the ball if someone in the other team brings them to the ground.

Rugby League rules state that a team can only be tackled six times before handing the ball over to the other team. In Rugby Union this does not happen. The players use maul and rucks (where they push each other) to try to win the ball.

Barrington Stoke would like to thank all its readers for commenting on the manuscript before publication and in particular:

Tahira Aniga
Sasha Brown
Rebecca Causer
Leah Carter
Arlind Celkupa
Peter Czinege
Olivia Follows
Stonie Griffiths
Emma Hadwin
Shakoor Islam
Monjur Jalloh
Saffet Kabaki
Jason Karanja
Niaz Khan
Fahima Khanom
Naimah Khatun
Joy Luc
Olivia Marsh
Micah McDowell
Tom McVeigh
Libby Quinn
Ethan Shortt
Matty Stelfox
Caitlin Wilson